MOTH & FLAME

GOTHIKA & THE BLACKSPIRE EMPIRE

CHIARA FORESTIERI

Illustrated by
VANESSA AMBRATA
Edited by
HUNTER HAMID

THANK YOU TO:

(PLEASE EXCUSE THE EXTENSIVE SWEARING. IT'S MY REDNECK WAY OF EXPRESSING MY FERVOR)

My children for tolerating my ridiculous working hours and bringing unfathomable love and joy to my life.

Hunter, my editor, without you, this book would have been an absolute mess of typos and grammatical errors that would otherwise have completely obscured our reader's ability to fully appreciate (and hopefully absolutely fucking love) this book. I fucking love you.

My ARC & Street Teams—you'll soon have your own dedicated section for me and all my [glorious] readers to worship you. Without y'all, no one would know about my books, my writing career would be nowhere, and all of my dreams would still be scattered in tattered pieces amongst the shards of what would have been a broken heart. You have helped make my dreams come to fruition, and for that, you will always have my eternal gratitude and undying love.

And Chris, for giving me the space to pursue my dreams unencumbered by the pressures of the world and thus

THANK YOU TO:

enabling my inspiration to run wild. I'd also likely be nowhere without you. I love you.

GRATITUDE

(SORRY, I PROMISE I'M ALMOST DONE)

Being on Read Me Romance podcast and the Moth & Flame audiobook would not have been possible if it weren't for my INCREDIBLE street team for bombarding them with requests for me to be on their show.

I LOVE YOU TO DEATH AND BEYOND. MERE WORDS WILL NEVER BE ABLE TO FULLY EXPRESS THE DEPTH OF MY GRATITUDE FOR YOU.

And that goes for you too, reader.

If you're interested in joining my ARC or Street Team for future works, please feel free to DM me or fill out one of the forms in my linktree on my insta: @authorchiaraforestieri or my TikTok (am far less active there).

I'd absolutely love to connect with you, as would our absolutely divine and loving members who are nothing short of effusive in all their love and support.

WARNING

If you are under 18:
my dear sweet, sweet child, please return this book and come
back when you're of age.

Additionally, if you do <u>not</u> like:
Copious amounts of seminal fluid
The FMC calling the MMC 'Daddy'
Explicit Sexual Content
or
Dom/Sub dynamics

This book is also not for you.

INTRODUCTION

THIS STORY HAS A TIME JUMP. Please note that this novella was written for a short form audiobook for the Read Me Romance podcast (THANK YOU, RMR! I LOVE YOU FOR GIVING ME THIS OPPORTUNITY!). The word limit for the audiobook was 10,000 words *and* there is a 'no death' rule… Don't worry *someone you will wish the worst for expires violently in book 2*.

Why am I explaining this? Because I want you to know why we leap from the FMC not having met the MMC to already being a few months into 'relations' with him. It was a necessary leap to take in order to close the distance between the beginning of the story and the HEA. Please, please, please take this into consideration when reading and (hopefully) leaving a review.

Outside of that, I highly recommend you check out Read Me Romance's podcast where you can not only listen to the Moth & Flame audiobook (coming April 2025), but also about a zillion other authors' delish and spicy audiobooks—

some of which include RUBY MOTHEREFFING DIXON, Kate Hunt, Liz Durano, and so many more. *fans self*

And lastly, THANK YOU. Thank you for giving me and my books a chance. You have my eternal gratitude and undying love. Because of readers like you, you have literally made my dreams a reality.

I love you.

— Chiara XO

GLOSSARY

Akash

(ah—kahsh)

The divine essence of the world that births, permeates, and destroys all things.

Blackspire Empire

The ruling body that governs all of Gothika

IOCI

acronym for inorganic cognitive intelligence. An operating system built into homes, vehicles, communication devices, etc.

Machina

(mah-kee-nah)

a hydro-powered automobile

Majori

(mah-jor-ree)

a magic wielder with substantial powers

Minori
(mih-nor-ree)
a magic wielder with 'lesser' powers

Nykanthros
(nye-kahn-thros)
a being that wields shadows and possesses a bestial form

Reaper
one of the elite within the Blackspire Empire's special forces division

Sanguinati
(sang — gwee—nah—tee)
an immortal being sustained by blood similar to the traditional 'vampire' but is not hindered by sunlight, is not allergic to silver, and will not die by a simple wooden stake to the heart.

The Exiled
Originally from a realm called 'Vallis Lacrimas' (The Valley of Tears), they are the first beings to arrive in Gothika—a once wild and verdant place, formerly known as 'Acheloria'.

Wielder
any individual or entity capable of wielding magic.

TRIGGER WARNINGS

If you find any of the following TWs disconcerting, please do not read this book. Begging is not beneath me. **I prostrate myself before thee, ye almighty reader, and humbly *beg* that you do NOT read this book.**

It is absolutely fucking soul-crushing to see negative reviews. Yes, I read them. All of them. Despite how it impacts my mental/emotional health and wellbeing (as it does for all authors). Not to mention, it makes the rating plummet and is there by a deterrent to people who might otherwise enjoy it. So when I see negative reviews that could have easily been avoided, simply because the reader didn't heed the trigger warnings or bother to look, and then they leave a scathing review because the trigger warnings upset them when the TWs are CLEARLY STATED, AND I LITERALLY BEG for you not to read the book if you don't like the trigger warnings…
It is nothing short of fucking excruciating.

Here are the TWs:

FMC calls the MMC 'Daddy'
(they have no actual familial relations, this is purely a
dom/sub kink)
Non-Consent
(between the FMC and another male character that is not
the MMC)
Spousal Abuse
(not committed by the MMC)
Mention of Stalking
(by the FMC)
Highly Explicit Descriptions of Numerous Sexual Acts
Cum Play
Cream Pies
Gagging
Knotting
Claiming/Marking
Dom/Sub Dynamics
Description of Violence
Discussion of Mental Health

If you can handle all of that we should be good on the rest.
Despite the dark TWs, this book is a fun, funny, and
heartwarming ride into an imaginative gothic/steampunk-y
realm.

For all those who have given their hearts to someone that didn't deserve it.

*If you haven't already, one day, you'll find your 'daddy' (or the right person to be 'daddy' for),
and thank the stars above that it never worked out with those that came before.*

HELLA

SIX MONTHS AGO

*M*y fiancé's cock pulses inside me as we drink from one another's veins. If it weren't for our Sanguinati venom, I wouldn't be able to achieve orgasm. Even as I do, it feels less like an orgasm and more like the sad flutter of a once-proud flag, now tattered and torn.

Love is for the poor because they have nothing else to live for.

My mother repeats those words to me every time I plead with her and my father not to force me into a loveless marriage with Alister.

To them, marriage is about strengthening allies, bloodlines, and fortunes—*not* love.

After a myriad of threats and curses sworn by my parents, our entire family, the entirety of the Blackspire Blood Vaults board, and seven months of procrastinating and desperately trying to escape my fate, I finally succumbed to the inevitable and accepted the engagement proposal to the so-called charming and charismatic Sanguinati male currently sliding his still-hard cock out of me.

I hadn't had high hopes, considering his family is notorious for their unsavory methods of conducting business, but they are wealthy and powerful, much like my own family—which is all that seemed to matter to them. Our engagement won't be publicly announced, nor our marriage, to assure my safety. My fiancé and his family have many enemies, and if they know who I am, it puts a target on my back.

As Alister's eyes lift to mine, there's no warmth or sign of the charm he so generously bestows on others. I've given him what he wants.

Blood.

And every time I give Alister my blood and my body, I feel less and less like myself. Like he takes a part of my soul with him every time he fills me with his cum and then silently leaves. Thankfully, I won't have to see him again until tomorrow morning. If I'm really lucky, not even until the following day because he'll be too busy with his morally depraved clients and distracted by his harem of mistresses.

Skin crawling with the need to rid myself of his *essence*, I wipe between my legs with a soiled sheet and lie in bed, waiting for him to shower and leave for work. With my eyes steady on the clock, time moves at a glacial pace. When the bedroom door shuts, announcing his departure, a heavy sigh escapes me. I finally rise out of bed, able to dress in peace without the weight of his soul-crushing presence.

* * *

EVERY DAY, my driver takes the same route to my office. As usual, numbness suffuses me as I stare out at the pristine steel, stone, and glass architecture that define our crowded, lonely city.

The singular bright spot amongst a palate of grey is the luminous, flame-filled glass sign reading *Moth & Flame*, framed by elegantly sculpted stone and opaque, mirrored windows. As ever, something inside me stirs at the sight of it, even with its foreboding wrought-iron doors.

When it first opened, only a handful of months ago, I'd searched on Spyder's Web to discover it's a *kink house*. Essentially, anyone over the age of two decades can show up and be *manually stimulated* by someone who will act out their kinks.

It's a rather ingenious idea. I imagine it saves many individuals from sexual repression and aggression, not to mention bringing fulfillment and intimate connection to the otherwise lonely populace of Dreadmere, Gothika's capital city.

Since I first laid eyes on it, I've secretly longed to go there —if only to meet its owner, Draven Morainu. Shrouded in mystery, not a single one of the detectives I hired could uncover anything about him. Eventually, I resorted to utilizing the only *colleague* my fiancé has ever introduced me to—Lazarus, Gothika's most nefarious crime lord, renowned for knowing everyone and everything about them—to help me find out who owns Moth & Flame and uncover any other *gems* he could find.

In the span of a single breath, I discovered *Draven Morainu* is a retired Reaper–one of the elite within the Blackspire Empire's special forces division–and an exceedingly rare being: *Nykanthros*.

One who wields shadows and possesses a bestial form. According to Lazarus, in Draven's case, his bestial form is some kind of monstrous Lykos creature that looks half-fae, half-giant wolf.

Lazarus grinned when he mentioned something about him being *a little older*. I recently faced my hundredth year, age is just a blur after that.

Now, I imagine you're asking, *"Isn't that mildly unsettling, stalker-ish behavior?"*

Without a doubt.

Do I care?

Not in the least.

Was it dangerous and reckless to visit the lair of Lazarus himself?

Abso-fucking-lutely.

Do I now owe him a favor because he refused my money?

Yes.

Am I terrified of when and what that favour will be?

Also, yes.

Was it worth it?

Fuck, yes.

My face is rather recognizable, and if anyone were to catch me patronizing a *kink house*, I'd probably be flayed by family, ostracized by the public, to then be brutally murdered by my horrid fiancé. Not because he gives a batty fuck about who I have sex with *or who manually stimulates me*, but purely because one of the few things he actually cares about is public perception.

Akash forbid I seek pleasure from anyone but him when he spends every evening glutting himself *and his cock* on his mistresses. A fact for which I am supremely grateful, as it allows me a brief reprieve.

So, in the shadows, I shall remain, admiring Mr. Morainu from afar.

My heart withers at the thought.

HELLA

PRESENT DAY

J lied. In the shadows, I did not remain. Did I mention I have very little impulse control? Hence, all the stalking of Mr. Draven Morainu. I tried to resist—really, I did. I spent months sneaking out of work and shirking my duties to haunt the vicinity of Moth & Flame, all in the hopes of catching a fleeting glance of the male. But it seems he rarely leaves the building—I've only caught him a handful of times. I can only assume he lives in one of the penthouses at the top of the towering stone-and-glass building.

When my patience finally dwindled away, I took the leap —conjured a disguise and slipped inside.

Draven is everything I've ever fucking dreamed of, even if I have to pretend not to know his name or anything about him. One of the numerous legal forms Moth & Flame clients are obligated to sign prior to membership states that all *Masters and Mistresses* of the house are forbidden from giving out their real names or personal details, to prevent any unwanted attention.

I am only ever allowed to refer to Draven as *Master, Daddy, My Lord,* or *Sir*—and for the last three months, I've spent nearly every evening after work sneaking into Moth & Flame in increasingly elaborate costumes, entering through VIP Members' discreet alleyway entrance reserved for their more affluent clients who prefer their predilections to remain private. *As they should.*

As unfathomable as it seems, I'm his only *personal* client. One evening, after yet another four-hour session, I tried to make a subtle comment by saying, *"Thank you for spending so much time with me. I'm sure you've had a very busy day with your other clients."* To my surprise, Draven replied, *"You're the only client I personally host."*

Each evening, our sessions are booked for one hour, and yet, by the time I leave, several hours have passed. I am also certain we've crossed a great many professional boundaries over the last three months, but much to my dismay, my *master* has yet to actually *fuck me.* Well, at least not with his cock. Or at least not the one attached to his body.

And while I have been on the receiving end of a very large, shadowy, lykos-shaped cock—bulging knot and all—I still haven't gotten to experience the real thing. *Much to my dismay.*

Tonight, however, I will beg. If you thought grovelling was beneath me, you are very much mistaken. And while, admittedly, there isn't anyone else in this realm I would get on my hands and knees for, there isn't a thing in this dreary, lonely world I *wouldn't* do for *Daddy Draven Morainu.*

Heaving a lovelorn sigh, I fix my gaze on the display screen where my singular photo of Draven lingers—a rather grainy image I managed to take myself when I'd just happened to catch him outside of his business. My mind travels to a time and place where I can escape my cursed fiancé, my foul family, and live a life beside Draven—if he'd have me.

My fantasizing is rudely cut short by an abrupt knock. My eyes reluctantly flick to the tall, blonde, slender silhouette I can see lurking beyond my office door: my sister.

Fuck.

HELLA

"*T*ell Lord Payne I don't give a fuck what he *assures* me of, I'm not interested, there's nothing he can do to change my mind, and I hope he dies in a fucking fire."

I did not spend the last century ensuring Blackspire Blood Vaults has ethically sourced blood just to have Lord Fuckhole ruin it all by becoming a major shareholder.

My sister, Leif, scowls at me as one would a naughty child. "You're being unreasonable."

My jaw clenches with frustration. "Have you tasted the blood from his cryovaults? I can *taste* the suffering. That male and his gods-forsaken enclave should be drawn and quartered in the Prime's square."

Leif pinches the bridge of her delicate nose. "You're forgetting the fact that some people *enjoy* the taste of suffering."

How could I fucking forget?

It's at least half the reason why my fiancé, Alister, is so fucking horrible. He *wants* to taste the misery in my blood every time he drinks from me. Every emotion has a very specific taste, and negative emotions, like misery, pain, and fear, add certain notes to the bouquet of flavors.

In our modern society, it's illegal to drink from someone without their consent. There are far too many people, not only humans, who would still be dwindling in population if our society's morals and the Blackspire Empire's legislation hadn't evolved to protect the *minori*—those with little to no magic-wielding abilities.

Still, there are many people who crave the taste of fear and despair in blood. People like my fiancé. *Akash damn him.*

As if Leif can read my mind, she adds, "*Like your fiancé.* He'll be furious if you decline Lord Payne's offer. House of Payne is his favorite."

I give her a curious look. "You say that as if it's a deterrent."

Leif rolls her eyes, tossing a pretty tendril of ash-blonde hair over a pale shoulder. "You know, I can't fathom what it is you have against Alister. He's charming, handsome, rich, *passionate—*"

My sardonic laughter cuts off her itemization of my sadistic fiancé's *winsome* qualities. Standing abruptly, I usher her to the door. "Leif, if you adore him so much, by all means, go and fuck him. In fact, I implore you. He's bored of his mistresses—one of them even *died.* A tragic accident, I'm sure. He's no doubt in dire need of your condolences. Do what you will with him, so long as you *decline Payne's offer.*"

Leif's brows lift with mild surprise as she fails to suppress the ghost of a grin.

I slam the door in her face. My anger is bright and hot, making my fangs ache with the need to tear someone's throat out, but when my eyes catch on the image of Draven on my screen, the fog of seething rage lifts from me like a cursed veil stolen by the wind and is swiftly replaced by a Draven-shaped duvet of joy and desire.

Tomorrow, my darling.

Because first—there are plans to be made.

My eyes settle on the shelf behind which lies a hidden safe containing the treasure trove of money and priceless jewels I've been secretly hoarding since my family forced me to sign my life away to a male who only wants me because I'm the largest shareholder in a company that owns forty percent of the blood bank market.

DRAVEN

$\mathcal{A}$s I approach the outskirts of Gothika's wealthiest neighbourhood, I flick off the headlight of my hydro-bike to conceal myself, no longer able to hide amidst the peppering of traffic as I discretely tail Hella's posh hydro-carriage.

My appointment with her isn't supposed to be until tomorrow, but my guts churn at the idea of her being left at the hands of her fiancé. She's never explicitly told me about his treatment of her, but it's written all over the scars on her pretty throat. While stalking her isn't exactly the height of professionalism...

Professional boundaries can get fucked.

So I've found myself haunting her every evening, whether or not we've had an appointment. Whether it's after she's already gone to sleep or just after she's left work, I don't go home until I've laid my eyes on her to see for myself that she's ok. Blessedly, her fuckhole fiancé is never anywhere to be found.

Whoever he is.

Yet another thing she insists on being discreet about.

Not that I have any right to complain. I haven't told her my name yet. I'm going to convince her to leave her godsforsaken fiancé first.

Thick, lush evergreens line the streets, and the mansions in between grow further and further apart. Finally, at the top of the hill that overlooks the city, I watch as Hella's hydrocarriage turns into an ostentatious driveway. A giant, illuminated fountain featuring half a dozen topless syrens demarcates the gated entrance, boasting curling, sharp, wrought-iron finials.

I park my bike deep within the foliage, waiting for her hydro-carriage to ascend the hilly, winding driveway that leads to a modern, gothic, castle-esque monstrosity that overlooks the city.

I reach the fence, further guarded by a powerful ward, but thanks to one of the many perks of being a Nykanthros, there are few barriers able to hinder my shadow form. I shift partially, slipping through effortlessly.

I'm still some distance from the front entrance of Hella's home, but with my heightened senses, I hear the shutting of the carriage.

"Thank you, Herman."

"A lovely evening to you, madame. *Akash's* blessings."

"And to you."

I reach the tree line nearest the front of her house just as she steps inside. A male servant shuts the door behind her.

Fuck.

My eyes scan the myriad of windows. I hold my breath, waiting for her bedroom light to flick on. Eventually, several windows to the right and up two stories, a set of balcony doors is illuminated. I jump, landing with a soft thud on the stone balcony. And there she is—my beautiful female—shedding her clothes.

She disappears through a doorway, and I follow her

across the gigantic balcony to a twin set of doors. They bless me with an unobstructed view as she climbs into the shower. My cock thickens, and my knot throbs as I watch her step beneath her waterfall shower. A distant part of me simmers with a sense of dread at the idea of her fiancé, very uncharacteristically, deciding actually to come home for once and walking in to find her. While I am not an impulsive male, even I have my limits. I can't say I'd have the self-restraint to stop myself from prying him off of her if he dared.

Thoughts of her betrothed disappear like dust in the wind as Hella begins to tease her breasts, her lips part on a soft moan, vaguely muffled by the windows.

A moment later, she sits on the marble bench of her shower, spreads her legs wide and begins to toy with her clit. The sight makes it painful to keep my steel-hard cock trapped within my trousers. I grip my pinned length, squeezing as if it will do anything to relieve me of the soul-deep ache I have for this female—in all ways. Not merely for her body.

Her hips give tiny thrusts as she teases the hardened, dusky tips of her breasts in tandem with her clit. *"Fuck, daddy, yes. Give me your knot."*

The last bit of my restraint snaps in twain as unparalleled satisfaction suffuses me.

She knows who she belongs to.

I am certain there's no one else besides me that she calls *daddy,* and based on the myriad of scents surrounding her home, not a single one of them is a being that would possess a knot.

Determined to cum with her, I unbuckle my belt and open the zipper of my trousers just enough to liberate my cock. My pre-cum is quick to drip in thick strings from my tip, and I don't hesitate to palm a handful of it and stroke it over my crown and length as I begin to pump. Hella's body is already tightening with her approaching orgasm, and I hasten my movements to follow her over the edge.

I'm so primed with blue balls from months of tending to her needs that, within less than a minute, I have to clench my teeth to stifle my growl as an orgasm builds at the base of my spine. A string of curses leaves Hella's lips as she works her clit at a frantic pace, and her back arches.

The hand gripping her left breast comes down to piston a finger into her tight, pink channel as she continues to caress her clit with the other. *"Oh, fuck, daddy... Yes!"*

The sight and sound are my undoing. My strokes along my weighty length stutter, and I use my free hand to work over my knot. A deep grunt escapes me as release paints the pristine stone tile of the balcony. I watch Hella writhe as her own orgasm consumes her. *"Fuck, fuck, fuck—"*

Yes, Hella. You belong to me.

Soon, I'm going to mark that beautiful pussy as mine.

HELLA

*H*e came for me *again*. My heart swells—*metaphorically, not physically*—to the point of pain at the sweetness of it.

Fuck me, I love him so much it fucking hurts.

So I decided to put on another little show to reward him. Perched on the bench in the shower, my senses are still tingling with the undeniable sensation of being watched. *By him.*

Every night since we've met, he's shown up. Sometimes even after I've fallen asleep, but his presence always stirs me. I can feel it in my bones. In the visceral ache taken residence in my chest–an ache that lights up every time he's near and weeps fiery tears when he's not.

If it weren't for the fact that the house staff—all of whom are *majori* and would easily sense his magic—would rat me out just to further ingratiate themselves with Alister, I'd have gone out onto the balcony and pulled him into the shower with me.

Such a transgression would end in my death. I have *zero* doubt.

Thankfully, Alister is out, as per usual, with his mistresses, and my mind is my own to visualize Draven claiming me as I pleasure myself.

I dare a glance out of the window, but with the lights on in the bathroom, I can't see more than a few feet onto the balcony.

We've maintained a shred of professionalism–something I have every intention of annihilating as soon as I manage to enact my plan to liberate myself from Alister and all things Blackspire Blood Vaults.

After rinsing off, I turn off the shower and reach for my towel. I should be able to *will* myself dry, but unlike Draven and a scarce few others, I'd only manage to leave myself damp. As I smooth my fluffy white bath towel over my skin, the sensation of his eyes on me is already reawakening my arousal and it makes me feel bold.

Striding to my bedroom, I shirk the towel from my body along the way. I climb atop my bed on hands and knees, positioning my ass to face the balcony window where I can feel Draven looming. My arousal is already slick and gooey between my thighs, having only just come and consciously not bothering to *dry* the area when I towelled myself off.

With two fingers, I spread my lips, sweeping through the wetness seeping from me to show him.

Look at what you do to me, Daddy.

After a few moments of circling my clit, I reach inside a hidden compartment within my bedside drawers and pull out the thick, knotted silicone phallus that looks nearly identical to the shadow of Draven's cock—the one that he fucks me with every session. I'd procured it recently, specifically for this occasion. It features a suction cup on the base of the knot.

I fail to stifle my grin as I saunter towards the floor-to-ceiling window separating us, lower myself to my knees, spit on the window like I'm fucking mad at it, and slam the suction cup of my dildo to the window with a definitive *thud*.

He must know I can see him.

Much to my dismay, this dildo doesn't leak Draven's precum, so I stimulate as much saliva as possible to make this as messy as I want it to be. I palm the large member, pressing a lush kiss to its tip as my eyes lift right to where Draven would be standing. My heart skips and thunders in my chest as my eyes latch onto his hulking silhouette.

I fucking love you.

Do you know that big, beautiful, fucking bastard?

There's no one else in this world for me but you, and I will gleefully claw the eyes out of anyone who dares to set their sights on you.

With the flat of my tongue, eyes locked on his silhouette, I drag a thick stripe along the dildo's length.

Fuck me, this silicone is dry.

I remedy that by welcoming it into mouth, pushing it as far back into my throat as possible, bobbing a few times to trigger my gag reflex. Tears leak from my eyes, and when I swiftly withdraw lest I vomit, there's a nice long, thick string of saliva connecting me to it. With a hungry hum, I stroke it over the length of it before I return it to my throat to repeat the action so I can press wet, sloppy kisses up and down the length as my closed palm works the crown to demonstrate to Draven my need to worship him.

The pounding pulse in my pussy seems to reach a crescendo, and I can't resist the demand any longer. Finally, I stand and turn, bending at the waist to position my pussy right in front of the dildo, still dutifully protruding from the window. I push my hips back, hands on my knees, forcing the crown to part my aching flesh and swallow the head of Draven's replicated cock inside me. It provides a formidable stretch that punches the air from my lungs.

With steady, short thrusts, I work the thick shaft inside me until I reach the knot at it's base and I realize there's no fucking way I'm going to get that to fit.

Draven will just have to do that himself.

Slipping one hand between my thighs, I create a steady rhythm, driving my hips back to stroke my spasming core along the length.

Through the window, I hear the distinct sound of Draven's grunt, and flick a glance over my shoulder to see his silhouette drawing closer. It's too dark to see for certain, but my mind procures the image of his fist pumping his cock. I imagine he's visualizing the same thing I am: burying himself inside me as he fills me with thick ropes of his cum to claim me as his.

Soon, my love, soon.

DRAVEN

$\mathcal{N}$ever in my life has my willpower been tested so thoroughly. It took everything within me not to pull Hella off the imitation cock and split her in fucking two with my own. I am filled with both satisfaction and the burning desire to bend her over my knee, smack her luscious ass until it's bright red and tender, and teach her a lesson for teasing me like this.

I painted her window with my seed, and rage blossomed in my chest at the fact that I had to *will* it away out of fear of her having to face her fiancé's wrath if he ever showed up to notice it.

Naughty fucking girl.

And tomorrow night, when she shows up for her appointment with me, so help me *Akash*, I'm going to convince her to leave him.

After I give her a thorough spanking.

HELLA

THE NEXT MORNING

"You fucking cunt. How dare you try to deny Payne's offer." My eyes close on a discrete sigh as the soul-crushing weight of Alister's presence settles upon my shoulders, and my chest. I'd slept so fucking peacefully knowing Draven was nearby, and Alister was out busying himself with his mistresses. I don't even offer him a glance, and merely continue to sift through our cryo-vault for my favorite blood before I head to my office. When I don't respond, Alister appears behind me, fisting the collar of my silk shirt.

"Unhand me at once, or I shall liberate you of the vile appendage."

Alister replies by burying his face in my neck and inhaling deeply before sheathing his fangs in my flesh. His bite is deliberately vicious. If I attempted to force him off me, I'd tear my own throat out in the process. *"I fucking hate you."*

Alister hums his pleasure against my throat in response. A moment later, the venom seeps in, eliminating the pain and causing arousal to burst through me like fucking dynamite.

Alister yanks my skirt up, and under the force of the venom, I only manage a feeble struggle that ends the moment his cock slides inside me and the swift build of my climax begins.

Draven, Draven, Draven. His name is a mantra in my mind.

Alister's fangs release me as he shoves me onto the white marble countertop. The blood from the ungracious wound trickles onto it, painting it red as he bends me over, and his thrusts turn sadistic.

No matter the cost, I will soon be free of you.

My eyes clench shut, and I visualize it's Draven's powerful form behind me. Gradually, my body relaxes, and another orgasm rises within me. A tremulous smile lifts my face, and the hatred tainting me bleeds away. A soft moan of pleasure escapes me as the vision of Draven becomes clearer. It's a balm to my soul until Alister fists my hair, pressing my face hard against the marble counter as he goes rigid behind me, filling me with his cum, and leaving my heart and soul more hollow than ever.

Alister slides out of me, tucking himself back into his trousers.

"Leif gave me the courtesy of notifying me of your betrayal. You *know* how I would feel if this deal fell through. Thankfully, the entire board outvoted you, and Lord Payne was remarkably forgiving and happy to proceed."

Seething, I tug my dress back into place. "I have spent my entire career trying to right the wrongs of Blackspire Blood Vaults, and ever since you—"

Alister throws his head back with a sardonic laugh. "Since I what, Hella? Since I saved your family's company, their entire legacy, from bankruptcy because of your misguided idealism? Your family would have *nothing* without me and my family."

Tears of righteous anger burn my cheeks as my hands tremble with the desire to tear Alister's head from his body. "Words cannot describe the depths of the hatred I have for you."

Alister huffs, rolling his eyes. "So you've said. I'm bored of you, Hella. So very, very bored."

With a deep breath, I push down my anger.

"Alister, please don't do this. Lord Payne *hurts* his donors. The male is a stain on our community, our people, and *our life's work.*"

"Gods, you're dramatic. Payne provides the best blood on the market. I don't know why you assume his methods of extraction are nefarious. Perhaps his donors suffer from depression. Is that his fault?"

"All of them, Alister? You really find it plausible that *all* the blood in his vaults is tainted—"

"Seasoned," Alister corrects.

—with virtually every form of suffering."

Alister gives me an incredulous look. "That's the best part. And I'm not the only one who thinks so. Did you even look at his revenue reports? *They're insane.* You should be thanking the gods he's merging with us."

My vision gradually turns red. Instinct screams at me to bleed him dry. Unfortunately, I have no doubt I would die if I tried. So the next best thing bursts from me. "I'm leaving you."

For the first time in our excruciating engagement, Alister's face slackens with shock, as if I've just slapped him in the dick. A moment later, his head tips back with raucous laughter. When he straightens, tears of amusement brim his eyes.

"Oh, darling—you're hilarious."

"I wasn't joking."

"Hella, if you truly think I'll ever let you leave, you're more delusional than I thought."

My blood turns to ice. "You're delusional if you think I'll stay. I'd rather die than spend the rest of my life with you."

A malevolent grin tilts a corner of his lips. "That can be arranged."

DRAVEN

"*A*rtemis, what time is it?" My house's IOCI—inorganic cognitive intelligence—replies a moment later in her cool, feminine voice. "Four p.m., my lord. You have two hours until your appointment with Miss Vex-Nocturni." My heart leaps with excitement. Every day, the moment that female sneaks into Moth & Flame dressed in a trench coat and moustache with her hair tied up inside that ridiculous fedora, it's the highlight of my fucking life.

Vale gives me a knowing grin. "Counting down the minutes?"

I spit a mouthful of blood onto the sparring mats. "Always."

Vale chuckles as warmth and appreciation glow in his eyes. He knows how I feel about Hella—and just how isolated a life I've lived. While polygamy is common practice among Sanguinati, I am incapable of sharing. Her engagement is the only reason I haven't told her how I feel—or given her my knot—despite the way my magic and my beast demand that I do.

"You sure you want me to keep bludgeoning you?"

Vale is a Sentient. Essentially, if a god and a robot could procreate and have offspring, you would get someone like Vale: a feeling, thinking, and creative being made up of inorganic flesh and blood that never tires, never needs to sleep, nor does he have any other biological requirements—although he can partake and quite enjoys doing so.

We only ever spar in my unshifted form, and I don't use my magic. It would be an unfair advantage and provides me more of a challenge. Today, I bested him in the first fifteen of our sparring rounds, but he's been handing my ass to me in the last five.

Drawing in a deep breath, I wave him forward, and he lunges for me. My side screams in protest as I force my muscles to contract, leaping forward to meet him and deliver a flying knee to Vale's perfectly sculpted face.

Thanks to my injuries and fatigue, he sees the move before it lands, weaving out of the way before nailing the other side of my rib cage with a devastating right hook.

Dropping to a knee, I finally raise a hand, followed by a swathe of shadows.

"*Match,*" Artemis swiftly declares. Her tone is ripe with both boredom *and* amusement. "Very good, sire. If you'd been fighting a human, they'd be thoroughly deceased."

Having served the Blackspire Empire since its inception nearly a thousand years ago, my combat skills are unmatched–as is my magic. An exceedingly rare advantage considering the fact that the populace of Gothika has faced dwindling control over their magic since The Exiled arrived.

Still, Artemis never misses a chance to make me the butt of a joke, and I wouldn't have it any other way.

Vale's lips twitch with restrained laughter as I send a bloody grin in the direction of one of her cameras. "Thank you, Artemis."

Vale swipes a thickly muscled arm across his forehead,

which only serves to smear his silver blood. "See you downstairs?"

I nod and turn to leave as Artemis chimes. "You've a new client today, Master Vale. Would you like me to read you the details?"

Vale retrieves a moist towel that Artemis has supplied in the dumbwaiter. "How long until they arrive?"

"Not until eight this evening, sir."

"I'll check my Spyder Mail later then. Thanks, Arty."

Artemis' voice turns sultry. "I live to serve, my lord."

Vale's brows lift as he directs a coy grin at the floor, speaking in a husky tone. "If only you had a body to worship, my darling."

Artemis hums her pleasure. "Perhaps, one day, I shall."

"If I lick the floor, will you feel it? Would it hasten your desire to join me?"

I shut the door, eager to escape their foreplay and make myself presentable for the female I can no longer deny is my *soulbound.*

DRAVEN

*A*fter returning from Hella's, I spent much of my morning and afternoon in a restless state of either sleeping, or stroking my cock into a gods-damned chafe. My female is driving me fucking mad. So much so that I can scarcely manage to focus on the administrative tedium Moth & Flame requires of me.

When I see Klaus is behind the stone reception desk with his assistant in the foyer of Moth & Flame, a wicked grin splits my face in anticipation.

Wherever Klaus goes, unintentional hilarity follows. He and his assistant are murmuring something I dutifully *pretend* not to hear as Klaus' eyes lift to mine over the rims of his tiny, circular spectacles. They're not even large enough to conceal the entirety of his eyes, and I have no idea why he bothers to wear them. But if the male is anything at all, it's eccentric.

The salt-and-pepper-bearded immortal, with the bald head dressed only ever in some variation of tight black leather, is richer than sin and has a phobia of germs and being touched. Why the fuck he would choose to provide kink release is beyond me, but you'll never hear me complain about it. He drives a solid thirty percent of Moth & Flame's revenue.

Shortly after I opened Moth & Flame, Klaus showed up, assistant in tow, and eager to patronize. The only problem was his kink was servicing others, and allowing a client to service other clients would raise all sorts of legal red tape. So I hired him. Within months, the male had become, quite literally, famous.

As if the thought alone cued a devoted patron's entrance, one of the double doors swings open, and in walks a pretty female. She squeals with delight at the sight of him and rushes towards the desk. I halt my forward movement, giving my own silent squeal of delight in anticipation of witnessing Klaus at his finest.

"Klaus! *Oh my gods, oh my gods, oh my gods!* I've waited for six months for this appointment, and you're finally *here!* I'm Layla! I've been *dying* to meet you!"

I *barely* succeed in suppressing my glee as I watch *Layla* extend her hand in the very human gesture of a handshake. I have to bite my cheek so hard it bleeds as Klaus bestows Layla with something that resembles a smile–like the wince of a too-hard-pinched nipple.

Klaus clears his throat, composing himself and *wills* a small prosthetic hand on a slender telescopic rod into existence. With careful precision, he gently places the fake hand in her hand for her to shake. His voice becomes a dramatic *coo.*

"*The pleasure is all mine, darling.*"

The delight on Layla's face falters as she hesitantly shakes the miniature prosthetic before she makes a high-pitched sound that I imagine is not too dissimilar to how she'll sound when he's providing his renowned *manual stimulation.*

No one knows exactly what that involves. Every one of

his clients signs an NDA that forbids them from divulging how he coaxes his clients into such intense orgasms they travel far and wide to be serviced by him. No one knows what type of immortal he is, where he comes from, or if his real name is even Klaus.

When Klaus releases the telescopic end of the prosthetic hand, his wraith assistant, Camilla, stands by with a bin. Layla looks up at Klaus with wide, adoring eyes. "May I keep it, Master Klaus?"

Having imbibed my dose of joy thanks to bearing witness to the bizarre interaction, I ascend the steps to my office to complete the finishing touches on the newest model of my Crypts & Chimeras character—a rogue female Sanguinati assassin that bears a striking resemblance to the female I've fallen head over heels in love with as I wait for her arrival.

HELLA

"This is by far the most disastrous idea you've ever had." I'm sitting across from my magistrate, Balthazar, who's peering at me from over the rim of his round, wire-framed spectacles.

"The only consequence that concerns me is that spending my life with Allister will be the death of me."

The delicate, bejewelled chain dripping from the stems of his glasses tinkles as he massages the bridge of his nose and heaves a sigh. "Darling, I admire your determination. Really, I do, but I'll fear for your life more if you try to leave him than stay with him."

"Balthazar, I'm fairly certain that once we do marry, it'll only be a matter of time until he disposes of me, just as he does his mistresses. I will not be dissuaded."

Balthazar's brows pinch in distress as he nervously twists the dramatic curl of his auburn moustache. "Darling, I'm sure that's not true. Come now, you can't say things like that about your future husband. The man is on the chair of numerous charitable organizations."

Truly, it's a testament to my self-restraint that flames don't spew from my nostrils on every exhale.

"I will not be dissuaded."

He shakes his hand in dismay. "I supposed as much. You're aware your family will likely disinherit you, and that you'll be voted out by every chair on the board of Blackspire Blood Vaults."

As much as I already knew it, hearing it aloud makes something in my heart fracture. Watery emotion burns my eyes, forcing them away from Balthazar's to the floor-to-ceiling windows of his office, overlooking the Dreadmere Grand—one of the few verdant sanctuaries amidst this stony city. My mind drifts to Draven, and my heartbeat lightens to pitter-pattering in delight of its own lovesickness. Stealing away the heartache over a family I could never trust and a company I've poured my life's blood into being taken from me.

Balthazar's voice bleeds with trepidation.

"Hella... You've got this peaceful look about you. It's terrifying."

Inhaling deeply, a sense of peace washes over me as the words rise to my lips.

"The board needn't bother with any vote. I'm resigning."

Balthazar's jaw falls so hard I'm surprised it doesn't hit him in the cock.

"Hella, surely there's an easier way? One that doesn't involve this grandiose self-sabotage."

I proceed to examine my crimson nails.

"If I've learned anything in life, it's that one must suffer an end in order to have a new beginning."

Balthazar splutters. "Darling, but—*please. Have reason.*"

Rising from my seat, hope swells bright and voluminous in my chest, like the rays of the rising sun painting the sky as it claims its victory against night. Regardless of the fact I may meet my own death in this endeavor, excitement bubbles inside me as my eyes pass over the sprawling city below and settle on Moth & Flame's facade in the distance.

"Balthazar, I need you to draft a letter declaring the dissolution of my engagement contract and my letter of resignation."

HELLA

The foyer of Moth & Flame is a toasty reprieve from the foul weather torturing the skies as I slip inside the alley entrance with a swipe of my key, satchel of jewels and cash in hand. Having finally arrived to my blessed reprieve, I heave a sigh of relief, setting my bag down to remove my absurd trench coat and hat. Moans and cries pepper the air, muffled behind the doors of the various kink rooms, whilst my heart flutters on wings of anticipation.

Just as I'm about to peel off the thick handlebar moustache, a large, calloused hand closes over my mouth, and a tall, thickly muscled body presses firmly against me from behind. A warm baritone voice in my ear. "What's a pretty little kitten like you doing all alone without her Master, hm?"

His head dips low, and I feel his mouth at the curve of my neck, spreading into a grin before he grazes his fangs against the sensitive flesh, making my nipples tighten on command. "Do you need to be punished?"

I give a muffled, "Yes, sir," through his palm. His hand moves from my mouth to my throat as the arm barred at my waist slips beneath my dress. A needy whimper escapes as he tugs my panties to the side and his fingers glide through my already-slick folds and over my clit. "Fuck, kitten, is all this sweetness just for me?"

"Yes, daddy."

Draven turns me around, dark eyes bright with desire and need. When his gaze dips to my moustache, dangling halfway across my mouth, I bestow a sultry grin. "I wore something special for you, darling. Don't you like it?" My tongue flicks out to tease the moustache for a split second before we both burst into laughter.

And that's all it takes for the weight of the world to lift from my shoulders. By the time our laughter slows, Draven has already pulled me against his chest, hands cupping my face as he stares down into my grinning, half-moustachioed face. He manages a gravelly hum through his chuckle.

"I wouldn't want you any other way, love."

My heart *swoons* like it's ready to swing right off the edge of a cliff and into Draven's big, strong arms.

Which is technically what I'm about to try and do.

Draven bows his head to gently tug the moustache the rest of the way off with his teeth before letting it sail to the ground. Our eyes linger, and time seems to suspend. The tension between us draws so tight, I want nothing more than to sag in his arms and beg him to kiss me.

It's been three months of this. I've fallen head-over-fucking-heels for this male. It's surreal that, technically, if it weren't for Lazarus—I wouldn't even know his name.

Draven's expression gradually hardens and as his hand fists a length of my hair in a way that bares my throat to him. My pulse ratchets higher as my arousal blooms when he brings his nose to my neck, nuzzling in a way that is pure dominance, heightened further as he nips and grazes my pulse point.

"Thank you for last night, love, but I have to admit. I'm

not entirely sure whether I want to punish you or reward you."

My heart stutters and pussy clenches at the memory as a grin glides across my face. It's the first time we're acknowledging the fact that he's been following me home every night, and it pushes us closer towards the last remaining boundaries between us that I so desperately want to demolish.

"Both?"

He draws back to hold my gaze. My eyes devour every hard plane and sharp angle of his face, the impervious, brutal strength and power his combat-honed body exudes. If he'd been hewn from marble, you'd think his creator had sought to wreak vengeance with each strike of the mallet. Yet the tenderness he consistently shows me—that crosses every line of professionalism—is enough to make me a puddle.

"So fucking perfect."

The words are murmured as if he's saying them more to himself than to me. This male is the sum total of every single one of my fantasies, and so help me, *Akash*, I'm going to make him mine.

DRAVEN

I can't take it anymore. After this evening's session with Hella, I'm going to ask her to leave her fiancé, whoever he is—she hasn't told me anything about him despite my very *unprofessional* prying—but I vow to slaughter him all the same.

Whoever he is, it's clear from the faint but jagged scars decorating Hella's throat that the way he feeds from her isn't done to give pleasure but to harm. When I'm finally able to coax his name from her lips, a violent demise shall be met upon him.

I can no longer deny who she is to me, and I know that she feels it too. I can fucking hear it in the pounding rhythm of her heart, singing its syren song to the beast in me.

Dressed in nothing more than the matte black silk robe I've provided, she's lying face down on the cushioned black leather kink table. Gradually peeling back the fabric of the robe, I reveal her thick, luscious ass that instantly summons my cock to grow thick and heavy with need.

Slicked with oil, I glide firm hands over the length of her

back, gradually feeding some of my shadows to assist in kneading and teasing her body to new heights even as the tension inside me continues to wind tighter.

When Hella first became a Moth & Flame member, I'd worn sterile gloves, but as this intangible thing between us grew and strengthened, we forsook numerous professional boundaries to the point where only a few remain: I still haven't told her my name, I haven't given her my cock, and I haven't kissed her.

Yet.

All three I have every intention of remedying this evening.

My palm comes down in three quick, firm slaps to one of the thick globes of her ass causing the flesh to reverberate in a way that makes me fucking salivate. Hella's nails dig into the table as she gives a wanton cry that makes my cock twitch with satisfaction.

"You know how much I fucking miss you when you're not here with me, Hella? And then you pulled that shit last night. Such a fucking cock tease, aren't you, princess?"

She doesn't answer. Merely wiggles her hips, arching her back as if to offer me her ass. I dole out the same punishment to her other cheeks to then admire the bright red prints of my hands on her ass that draw out my growl of pleasure.

"Answer me, Hella. Are you daddy's little cock tease? Trying to turn him into a rabid fucking animal."

She finally gives me a whimpered, *"Yes, daddy,"* as her hips give another wiggle.

"Give me this fucking cunt." My words come out little more than a growl as I yank her hips off the table and position her on her knees.

The action reveals her tight, puckered hole to me as the glistening pink folds of her pussy part, and I can't resist the urge to spank *her* too. She yelps, ass jiggling and core clenching.

"Why, Hella? Tell me why you had a replica made of my shadow's cock, and maybe I'll reward you."

She hesitates only for a breath. "Because I want you. I want you to claim me. I want you to *own* me."

My heart nearly bursts with emotion as my cock *weeps* with joy.

At the first graze of my fingers teasing her slit, her back arches to steal more contact. She's rewarded with another smack to one of the plump globes of her ass.

"Yeah, baby? That's what you want? You want daddy to protect you and take care of you? Claim you as mine?"

"Yes, daddy, please. I need you."

As much as I want to lay it all out on the table here and now, I also don't want lust clouding her judgment. I want her to be thoroughly sated so she can make a clear-headed decision.

With a growl of satisfaction, I send a thick tendril of shadow to lick her entrance. "You do love to be such a good girl for me, don't you?"

She lets out a soft cry, red nails digging into the cushion of the table. *"Yes, sir."*

Pre-cum leaks from the head of my cock as my knot throbs with need to fill her. Among my kind, a male's knot is reserved solely for his *soulbound.*

My hands soothe away the sting of her reddened cheeks, squeezing their heft firmly. The movement parts the delicate pink petals of her cunt further and the sight makes claws prick my fingertips as my beast surges towards the surface.

"Oh my fucking gods, Hella."

On an impulse to mark her cunt with something of my own, I summon a ball of saliva to spit on it before burying my face in my favorite place in the whole fucking world. Hella cries out as my tongue works every inch of her ass and pussy until I feel her body tightening at the approach of release.

Her breath catches when I pull away, and my shadows turn her onto her back. Throat and face flushed, there's a hint of vulnerability in her gaze —as if I might suddenly find something I don't like about her.

Impossible.

Hella could ask me to eat her clipped toenails, to which I'd reply, *"Be a doll and pass the salt."*

My shadows possessively grip Hella every which way: splaying her thighs, circling her waist, teasing her nipples, collaring her throat, and now, slicking against her entrance. Hella's hips begin to counter the work of my fingers as her eyes roll back, back arching, and she sweetly moans. *"... Need you."*

My heart squeezes with emotion I've never felt.

"I need you too, kitten."

Hella's eyes snap back to mine, lips parting at the fervor in my words. My shadows curl around her wrists, pinning them above her head, and splay her thick thighs wide, pinning her knees to the table on either side of her waist.

With a breathy whimper of desperation, her head cranes downward to watch as my shadows billow between her legs, further spreading the lips of her pussy. I *will* a portion of my shadows to take on the precise shape of my cock, slicking it through her folds from entrance to clit. She gives a soft cry, eyes rolling heavenward, her head tilting back. Tears leak from her eyes as she writhes beneath me.

"Oh, gods... daddy, yes."

It takes a herculean amount of restraint not to immediately bury my *actual* cock in her tight, pink cunt, drenched and dripping with need, as I silently deliberate whether to just make my demands of her now and claim her in every way our bond demands.

My shadow gradually pushes inside her with progressive thrusts that stretch her as she adjusts and spasms around its girth. Fixing her eyes to where the shadow of my cock splits her, soft keening sounds and unintelligible curses escape her throat. Her expression–a helpless pout in her state of overwhelm.

"Fuck, fuck, fuck, fuck—"

A growl of pleasure rumbles in my chest, even as my cock weeps its neglect, still strangled in the confines of my trousers.

"Such a good fucking girl. Look how beautifully you take my cock."

We both wish it were the cock attached to my body and not its shadow.

Soon. She needs to be coherent when she makes her decision, I have to remind myself, resisting my beast's demand and *soul-bound* needs.

Hella gives a vigorous nod, eyes lifting from her cunt to my gaze.

"Please. I want it so badly. I need it."

Her meaning is clear. The singular thread that restrains me is that of her fucking *fiancé.* Despite not even knowing his name, I've never wanted to murder someone so badly in my life. I don't dare fulfill our bond if she won't leave him. And I will not influence her decision under the influence of lust. I *will* however give her a taste of what she wants.

Her eyes widen as I ease my cock out from where it's trapped against my thigh, and give the aching flesh a firm stroke. Pre-cum swells and drips in thick strings from my broad crown to the floor. Hella's tongue slicks across her lips as her eyes return to mine.

"Can I swallow you, daddy? Please?"

My knot pulses in agreement despite my rule of never cumming before her.

Though teasing her…

"Just a taste, kitten."

HELLA

$\mathcal{T}$he sight of Draven's long, thick cock leaking voluminous amounts of pre-cum sparks a primal and soul-deep need to have him fill me with his knot and his seed. The vehement desire is only further spurred by the throbbing ache in my chest, entirely separate from the pounding of my heart, yearning to devour every part of him.–his saliva, his blood, his cock, his cum.

As though it's my first time seeing him—*it's not*—my eyes hungrily savor Draven's thick, bulbous crown where his arousal seeps in copious strings; every plump vein decorating his shaft; and the bulge of his knot.

"Give me your tongue, sweetheart."

The shadow of Draven's cock continues to languorously thrust in and out of me as he fists his cock and slaps it gently against my offered tongue. With a breathy moan, I greedily lick, suck, and kiss every drop of pre-cum from his crown as if it were my sole source of sustenance.

"Fuuuuccckkkk. Gods damn it, kitten."

Draven slides deeper into my mouth, fisting my hair and fucking my throat with the same languorous pace as his shadow works my pussy, all while the fingers of his free hand steadily stroke my clit.

Draven's gaze holds mine as tears slip from the corners of my eyes. His words come out little more than a frustrated growl.

"So fucking perfect. You know that? Tell me you know it, Hella."

My reply is far too garbled by his dick in my throat to be understood, but I take satisfaction in saying them none-theless.

"I fucking love you."

Gently stroking my jaw with his thumb, Draven's brows knit together before growling a curse and suddenly with-drawing from my throat. My breath catches as he moves between my thighs to tug my hips to the end of the table. His mouth licks hot stripes along my folds as his shadowed length pumps in and out of me before he settles over my clit, lavishing it with steady flicks of his tongue.

Still, my heart clenches at his lonely cock even as my orgasm begins to rise again. *"But what about you?"*

Draven's lips scarcely lift to murmur his reply.

"You already know you always come first, love. In every way."

It's too late for me to argue—tingling energy swells like a rising tide. Every muscle in my body coils tight, and I can't help but take a fistful of his hair, perching myself on one elbow to watch as the male of my fucking dreams devours me. That ache in my chest burns, demanding that this male mark me as his with his fangs, his cum, his knot.

"I want you—I need you. Need you to mark me as yours."

Draven's large hands grip my thighs hard enough to bruise. A snarl rips from his throat, muffled by his mouth's ministrations, as his eyes lift to meet mine. His lips wrap around my tingling bud, and he *sucks,* setting my body and world ablaze.

"Oh, gods, Draven, fuck! Yes!"

My throat tightens as if trying to snatch back the words. *Oh, fuck, I'm not supposed to know his name.*

Surprise widens Draven's gaze as I cry out and writhe beneath him from the force of my orgasm. He doesn't falter in his ministrations, continuing to suckle my clit, easing me back down into my body. When the spasming of my core ceases, his fangs graze the sensitive flesh of my inner thighs.

My heart pounds as anxiety coils in my gut. *How do I talk my way out of this?*

His voice is a quiet but warning rumble, that reminds me of the beast lurking inside him. "How do you know my name, Hella?"

As a former Reaper, it would take nothing for him to kill me, but intuitively, I know I can trust Draven with my life.

Though, it seems to strike me only now just how little I actually know about him. Anxiety fists my chest as I try to come up with a response. Despite the fact that he has been following me home every night to keep a protective eye on me... We hadn't even *met* when I'd started stalking him. And considering there's literally zero information to be found of him on Spyder's Web, the only explanation of how I know his name is that I did some serious snooping— something I'd always planned on *eventually* telling him about, but this...

"I... I..."

Draven straightens, tucking away his still-hard cock. The absence of his warmth, his touch, makes me shiver against the chill. When I try to close my legs and cover my breasts with my arms, his shadows hold me fast to the table, making a tendril of icy fear lick up my spine.

Oh gods, how do I tell him I stalked him and bargained with an infamous crime lord to give me information about him?

"You what? I need you to tell me the truth, Hella."

Panic has the words clawing up my throat, unceremoniously spilling my shame into the space between us.

"I stalked you."

Fire licks my cheeks and throat alongside a shocking swell of sudden emotion. No matter the fact, he's stalked me too, the fact that I did it to him when I'd never even met him and went to such great lengths to learn more about him, makes me cringe with shame.

Gods damn it, I should just let him kill me.

Draven's brows lift in surprise, and further explanation rushes out of me. "I saw you... Just after Moth & Flame opened. I searched Spyder's Web to find out what it was and to find... *you.* When I saw it was a kink house, I was terrified to risk coming here because of all the repercussions of someone catching me, so when I couldn't find any information on you... I..."

My eyes dare a glance up from the hole I've been burning into the floor with my shame up to his face—an utterly blank mask.

"You...?"

A tear streaks down my cheek as my gaze collapses beneath his cool stare.

"I hired someone to find out your name and your history for me."

His brows pinch as he scrubs a hand down his jaw. "Why?"

Incredulous, my eyes leap back up to his. *"Why?"*

Draven's vacant stare provokes my tears further. I've never seen him look at me with such a cold expression.

"Because I was *drawn* to you. *Compelled* by you. And I never feel anything for people in that way. I tried my best to ignore it, but I couldn't. I thought maybe if I could find out who you are, come to know some fragment of you–even if only from afar–that I'd be able to move on with my life. But I couldn't because I love you, you idiot! I've loved you since the moment I laid eyes on you! I would leave work early just in the hope of being able to watch you come and go—"

My half-sobbed words are cut short by my yelp as Draven suddenly shoves his face inches from mine, eyes darting between each of mine.

"Say it again."

I sniffle, trying to stifle the sob clawing its way up my throat.

"I love you?"

Draven's eyes slip shut, and the shadowy binds around my wrists and ankles finally give way as his hands capture my face, and he presses his forehead to mine.

"Again."

Relief washes over me like a fucking tidal wave.

"I love you, Draven Morainu."

A soft smile perches on his perfect lips.

"I love you too, Kitten."

DRAVEN

*W*ith eyes squeezed shut to quell their burning, I throw Hella over my shoulder. She yelps in surprise, attempting to cover her exposed ass and pussy as I march my way to the lift that will take me to my penthouse above Moth & Flame. She's rewarded with a swift smack to the voluptuous cheeks I'm moments from sinking my fangs into.

"Wait! Where are we going?! You have to take my bag!"

"My home."

My shadows grasp her leather bag, following us inside the elevator.

"…What if I'd been an assassin or something?"

My deep chuckle rumbles from me.

"Kitten, even if you were, my life is yours to take."

The lift's glass doors close, swiftly carrying us 45 floors into the sky. I've spent years slaving away for the Blackspire Empire, eliminating threats posed to the public and our democracy. Now, centuries later, I've finally broken free.

I've taken a lot of care to ensure my identity remains

hidden, living in relative peace. The fact Hella had been able to simply *hire* someone to find out who I was is deeply unsettling. It also means that whoever she paid already knew who I was. She'll tell me who, but they'll need to be dealt with, lest the hierarchs of Blackspire–or any of my former enemies–find me.

But first, I'm going to claim my *soulbound.*

The lift's glass doors face the outside world, and my eyes scan the bird's eye view of the city before us. I'd set this entire city ablaze to protect Hella. The elevator gives its haunting melodic cathedral organ chime, and the doors reveal the open-plan space of my penthouse foyer and living room. I stalk through to march us down the hall to my bedroom.

My heart gives a beautifully painful squeeze as I lay Hella across my bed. The sight of her naked and nestled safely against the dark duvet tugs at something in my chest.

Hella tugs nervously at her lip as she stares up at me.

"You have a beautiful home."

Still standing above her to savour the sight, I don't dare crawl onto the bed with her until I've made my demands and she's given me her decision. While I seek her approval in all things, there is only one thing on my mind.

"I want you to leave your fiancé."

A watery grin splits across her face. "I already have."

My breathing stills as emotion rises.

"Truly?"

She nods, tears slipping. "I visited my magistrate today. He's sending Blackspire Blood Vaults my resignation and my *ex*-fiancé a notice of dissolution for our engagement first thing in the morning."

In the next moment, I'm pulling her against my chest as I lean back against the headboard. She chews on her cheek, trying to tame her emotions as more tears spill, and I can't help but kiss them away.

"I want you to know that I never loved him. My family and their business partners forced the engagement upon me. My fiancé has no love or loyalty for me. He has only ever proven to be as cruel as his family."

I hadn't thought it possible to desire this male's death any more than I already do.

"Who is he?"

"Alister Belmont."

That slimy fucking weasel?

Rage summons the beast inside me upon learning this precious female was forced into the vile arms of *Alister Belmont* —a male that I have met on more than one occasion and have fantasized about killing every time our paths crossed. The only reason I hadn't killed him was the fact that he is under the protection of the Blackspire Empire—*my former employer.*

Stealing Hella for myself will have repercussions, but there is nothing I wouldn't sacrifice for her. And nothing will stop me from killing Alister Belmont now.

"Do you know him?"

The question takes a moment to reach my distant, whirling mind.

"I do."

Hella curls tighter into my arms as I stroke soothing circles on her back and press a kiss to her forehead.

"Then you know there will be consequences to me trying to escape him... dangerous ones."

"Yes."

"And you would still want to be with me?"

Hooking a finger beneath her chin, I draw her gaze to mine.

"Hella, I've spent my whole life killing for a living. What's a little more spilled blood when I'd forge a river of it just to lay my eyes on you?"

Does she really not know who we are to each other?

My chest swells with determination as I finally speak aloud what I've known and held back for too long.

"You're my soulbound, Hella. My life and my fate are yours, and so they shall remain."

Her throat works on a rough swallow as she slides an arm over the back of my neck, fingers threading into the short length of my hair as she holds my gaze.

"Alister will try to take everything he can from me: my fortune, my livelihood, my reputation—my life if he can find me—but my heart, my body, my soul—they are eternally yours."

A fervor unlike anything I've ever known consumes me as I spread her out beneath me and settle myself between her legs. My beast's claws slide free as my form shifts—growing in height and breadth. My trousers and shirt are reduced to ribbons in seconds.

Hella's eyes widen in awe as the scent of her arousal overwhelms my senses. My Nykanthros form looks like an unnatural thing conjured in nightmares and fairytales. While I grow to the terrifying size of a Lykos, fur sprouts along my back in a thick pelt as my face and body take on a monstrous melange of both fae and wolf features.

Very few have seen my beast's form and lived to speak of it. Not that I'd want them to. Other than my mother, *Akash rest her soul*, there isn't another soul in this realm who would describe me as anything other than an abomination.

And yet, Hella's eyes pass over me with nothing short of adoration. *"You're beautiful."*

A low growl builds in my chest as I *will* my claws to recede to fist her hair in one hand, tugging to better expose the delicate flesh of her throat. The voice of my shifted form is an even deeper, gravelly version of my own. *"And you're mine."*

My magic whispers over her skin just as I gently sink my fangs into the side of her neck. Satisfaction is another growl in my throat as I finally get to heal the numerous faint but ragged scars from Alister's vicious bite marks. It's something I've longed to do since the day I laid eyes on her.

She gasps against the sensation, body arching into mine as she cries out, her arousal scent thickening. Her blood spilling down my throat is intoxicating, euphoria that causes my cock and my knot to swell and harden to the point of pain.

My hips give a mindless thrust against her, painting her pussy and abdomen with my leaking seed. Hella reaches between us to give my length a teasing stroke that sends a jolt of electricity up my spine before aligning it with her entrance. She wiggles her hips, easing me inside. The sensation feels as if *godfire* has set my veins aflame. My fangs burst free as a frenzied snarl tears from my throat.

The look in Hella's heavy-lidded eyes soothes the beast in me as she strokes my jaw. *"Shhhh, I'll be full of your cum soon, my love. I'm yours."*

My claws prick her skin as I pin her hips in place, gradually pushing forward until my crown breaches her tight, slick entrance. My cock is even larger in this form, and it would be selfish not to take care. Thankfully, her pussy is already primed, thanks to my shadows and earlier efforts just minutes ago in Moth & Flame.

My shadows bloom around us, teasing her clit and the tight peaks of her breasts as I sit back on my heels to gaze at where we are joined.

Fuck, I've made a mess of her.

Thick puddles of my pearlescent pre-cum glisten against her skin, urging my hips into a steady thrust that eases my length deeper. I'm mesmerized by the way the pink petals of her petite cunt stretch and mold around my intrusive girth.

Within moments of my quickening pace and deeper strokes, Hella's nails bite into the flesh of my thighs, her jaw slackening. A cry escapes her, her back arching, her lush tits bouncing.

My strokes turn punishing as the beginnings of my own orgasm lick up the base of my spine, demanding I bury my knot inside of her.

"Oh my gods, Draven... Yes, yes, yes!"

"That's it, sweetheart. Milk this cock. I'm gonna fill this pussy up with so much fucking cum, she'll be weeping with it for a week."

"Yes, Daddy, please!"

My eyes briefly roll into the back of my head as my growls turn to grunts. At the end of each thrust, my knot coaxes her entrance, and I press harder each time. Hella's breath becomes keening, panting gasps as it finally begins to nudge inside. She props herself up on her elbows to watch.

My knot glides further—almost to the widest point. *So close. So fucking close.*

Hella's gaze returns to mine, brows pinched with need.

"I need it, Draven. Give me all of you."

As if to punctuate Hella's demand, my knot finally slips all the way inside, and I'm buried to the hilt. The bond between us thumps with a pulse of its own alongside the war drum of my heartbeat. Another snarl tears from my throat as Hella cries out, her pussy milking my cock of thick, hot, pulsing ropes of cum. My strokes become languorous.

"I fucking love you, Hella..."

Emotion slips free from her eyes, prompting me to close the distance between us. I brace myself on my elbows, framing her head.

"And I'll thank Akash every godsdamned day that you stalked me."

A watery grin splits her gorgeous face as she gives a surprised laugh.

"You don't think I'm insane?"

I chuckle, my nose grazing her temple before I plant a kiss on her forehead.

"Kitten, it's one of my favorite things about you."

HELLA

LATER THAT EVENING

I've spent my life hiding from everyone I know. Born amongst vipers, I never felt safe enough to express anything other than righteous anger or disgust. And now, I've been given the gift of Draven Morainu.

I've never been much for religion or its zealots, but I will thank *Akash* every day for uniting me with my *soulbound*.

Even if he is leading me back into the lair of Lazarus—the infamous underground crime lord who gave me Draven's name. As it turns out, Lazarus has many allies, including Draven. Little did I know, Lazarus was once a Reaper alongside him—many years before Draven retired.

Dark, busted-out windows observe us like haunted, hollow eyes as I scan the abandoned buildings lining the cobblestoned street. Draven, with me moulded to his back, cuts the engine of his motorbike and steers us to the entrance of the same warehouse I visited only months ago.

"There are only two people in this world I would trust with my life outside of you. Lazarus is one of them."

Still...

"This place is even creepier at night."

Draven chuckles. "I brought you for one reason, or else I'd have come alone."

"Why is that?"

"I want his golems to see you. To know that you belong to me and that you're a friend of Laz's."

A shudder runs through me. *Golems.*

"But why?"

"They are his eyes. They have a hive mind and are everywhere in this city. Under Laz's orders, they haunt the same nightclubs as Alister and the other serpents slithering around the underbelly of this city. If they see that you are my *soulbound* and an ally to Laz, they'll always keep an eye out for you too. You're safe, Hella. They'll be another measure of security. If Alister so much as speaks your name, they'll know about it."

My stomach churns even as I steel myself. Draven pats my thigh, signalling me to slide off his bike. He follows, pulling me against his chest. Large hands frame my face as he presses a lingering kiss to my lips.

"Nothing will happen, kitten. Lazarus will lure Alister to me, and then he'll be too fucking dead to raise a hand against you."

Draven takes my hand, leading me to the warehouse entrance. My heart leaps into my throat as two golems step out of the shadows—or *thin-fucking-air*—and open the double doors wide for us.

Shafts of moonlight spill through the cavernous ceiling as we're led by another golem. They're increasingly rare beings, supposedly animated not by soul but entirely of magic. My eyes roam across the sprawling interior of the warehouse, bouncing from one golem to the next. Some stand sentry, others unpack strange artifacts, while others weave ancient magic through the air and bring new golems to life.

It would take an inconceivable amount of magic to

sustain such a large army of golems. Access and control over that kind of magic hasn't been possible since before The Exiled founded Gothika & the Blackspire Empire.

As a Sanguinati, I should be able to *will* a goblet of blood into my hand as easily as pouring one. Instead, I am only able to manually pour one, like any other *minori*—a being with lesser magic.

But seeing Draven's magic, and now Lazarus', makes me wonder if perhaps magic is returning to Gothika.

The golem leading us comes to a stop, silently gesturing us towards a large table draped in black velvet and cluttered with artefacts; a glowing amber orb floats from above.

Behind it stands the notorious crime lord we've come to see. With the exception of his gold prosthetic arm, Lazarus is covered head to toe in tattoos. His eyes blaze an unnatural shade of gold—a color that very nearly matches the preternatural shade of his skin and slightly darker hair. His otherworldly beauty is a contrast to the coldness carving his features—until a knowing grin slides across his face to reveal a glittering smile and gilded fangs. His deep voice holds the warmth of the sun as he rounds the table to stand in front of us.

"What a pleasure to see the two of you. *Together.*"

I can't help but grin. "Yes, thank you for all your... *assistance.*"

Lazarus' lips twitch with amusement as he extends his gilded synth hand towards us. "My pleasure."

Draven embraces it with both hands. I'm surprised they don't embrace in that typical, back-clapping male way. After all, this is one of three people Draven trusts.

I don't miss the subtle tension in Draven's muscles as I accept Lazarus' handshake, nor does Lazarus. Both wearing unreadable expressions, but before any suspicion can grow, Lazarus endows us with another dazzling smile.

"Congratulations, Morainu. I have to admit, I envy you."

Draven's arm is a comforting weight over my shoulders. My eyes slide up to see Draven's reaction, and I'm surprised to see a look of unmistakable sadness. Lazarus flexes his hands at his sides, and I notice his flesh-and-bone hand is covered in a glove made of fine, silvery chainmail.

"I take it you've come here to discuss Alister."

My eyes leap from Lazarus' hands to his eyes, making my cheeks flush at being caught staring. Lazarus offers me a reassuring smile as Draven replies.

"You're still in close contact with him?"

Lazarus smirks, leaning against the table with arms folded and ankles loosely crossed. "Unfortunately. The male is a thorn in my side."

"I need you to set up a meeting with him."

Lazarus studies my reaction before gradually nodding.

"Consider it done. I just need to tie up a few loose ends… before any unfortunate accident befalls him."

My anxiety surges. "He's going to send every sentry in Blackspire looking for me. As will my family when they hear from him—"

Lazarus gives me a look that tells me he knows Alister better than I do. "No. He won't."

"But… *How?*"

A knowing grin curls a corner of his mouth. "What does Alister value above all else?"

My brows pinch. "Power? Money? Public opinion—"

Lazarus's smirk blooms wide as he taps one gloved finger on the tip of his nose. My jaw drops as relief and hope wash over me.

"Thanks to my golems and all of my night clubs' security footage, I have decades of visual documentation that reveal not only Alister's *methods* of conducting business but also depict him in numerous compromising *situations.*"

My brows leap, and the sympathy that softens Lazarus' features makes me question just how nefarious this male actually is.

"Look, I don't know how well you've come to know your husband or his family's way of doing business, but I can assure you, if any of this information were *leaked*, the Blackspire Empire's justice system would face collapse. Alister and his family would be hunted down."

At my slack-jawed expression, Draven smoothes my hair back and presses a kiss to my head, his voice a soothing murmur at my temple.

"See, kitten. Everything's going to be fine."

I frown. "Won't that put you in a compromising situation when he learns you have all this dirt on him?"

"Alister already knows. I will simply remind him and tell him that you are under my and Draven's protection."

My eyes dance between them in disbelief. "But won't he— or his whole family—hunt *us* down for threatening them?"

A grin saunters across Lazarus' face, and for the first time since I've met him, I get a glimpse of the malice I've heard horror stories about glinting in his otherworldly eyes. "They are certainly welcome to try."

Laz's eyes slide back to Draven as they seem to have another silent conversation. "Never a better time than the present."

My stomach knots as I glance between Lazarus and Draven.

"Pardon?"

Draven turns me into his chest, his gaze searches mine, causing unease to swirl in my gut. "Lazarus and I aren't from here."

My brows knit together. "Here as in… Dreadmere?"

"Here as in… Gothika."

My jaw drops. "You're from another realm?!"

Apprehension bleeds into Draven's eyes as he nods. "You're familiar with The Exiled?"

Did I say my jaw dropped? *It's now sailing towards the lowest circle of hell.*

GILDED FANGS & MORTAL FLESH

BOOK TWO | GOTHIKA & THE BLACKSPIRE EMPIRE | MAY 2025

Continue for a sneak peek…

*please note, book two is still a WIP and the following chapters have not yet been edited, so if you run into a few (or several) typos, I beg your forgiveness.

FAWN

"*H*ow do you feel about being restrained?" The orc male, Thalion, sitting in front of me, left a few parts of the form unanswered. As I look up from my tablet, he scrubs a hand down his handsome, tusked face. The twisted side of me gives an internal squeal of delight at the sight of his obvious discomfort. While I only have mildly sadistic tendencies, I do so love unlocking new kinks for big strong males that have a reticence to relinquishing control... because most of the time, that's exactly what they need.

After a moment, finally gives a grunt of ascension. "I'm not entirely sure, but I suppose I'm open to trying new things. Or at least my therapist says I need to be." Thalion's eyes steal glances at my veiled and robed form as if waiting for me to finally reveal what I'm wearing underneath. The robe is white silk and so deliberately oversized that the shape of my body is almost entirely indiscernible.

I offer him a patient smile before returning my eyes to his form, scanning the rest of his preferences. "Excellent. Would you prefer to underdress yourself, or would you like me to undress you?"

Tharion's throat works on a visible swallow. His dark tongue sweeps out over his full lips in a nervous action, and I have to suppress my giddy grin. *Oh, you dear, sweet, sweet boy. We are in for a treat.*

For all his bulk and masculine energy, there is a certain innocence about him that makes my toes curl in the best way.

"Uhm… I guess you can?"

My grin widens as I set my tablet down on my desk—the least kinky thing in my kink room other than the petite waste bin beneath it—as I saunter over to him and untie the sash at my waste. His breath hitches as I allow the garment to slide off my shoulders and pool at my feet. I'm wearing the white bridal lingerie set he requested; gossamer white veil included. The edge of which teases the tops of my ample bosom.

I allow him to look his fill for several moments, savoring the way the long, thick length of him bulges through the leg of his finely tailored trousers. He curses under his breath as my fingers drift upwards tease my nipples from beneath the little scrap of fabric draped over them from the cut-out underwire brassiere I'm wearing.

My eyes catch on the wet spot forming on the pants, where I can very clearly make out the thick crown of his cock.

"You're pleased…"

He gulps again, nodding. "Yes, ma'am."

My belly flutters with delight. I've always been a sucker for good manners.

"May I see the back?"

I can't help but giggle at his polite way of asking. "You may."

Turning, I arch my back a little to enhance the view he has of my ass and thighs framed and slightly overflowing over the edges of the lacy white garter belt, thong, and stockings.

Tilting my head over my shoulder, I peek at him from beneath my lowered lashes. His hands fist at his sides as if he's trying desperately to restrain himself.

Rotating to face him, I crawl onto this lap, straddling his thick muscular thighs. The male is enormous, and I feel like a pixie seated in his lap despite my above-average human female height of five feet ten inches. The position nearly brings us eye level, though I still have to tilt my head up to link into his sparkling dark eyes. There is a definite innocence and vulnerability there that makes my heart squeeze for this male. I do so hope he finds his mate. There is a palpable tenderness about him that softens my edges.

And if it weren't for the impenetrable fortress surrounding the tattered remains of my heart and the professional boundaries I have to maintain, I could see myself, in another life, liking this male. Instead, as I stroke his jaw, I only feel compassion for him the way I do for most people. There is no crackle of fire or electricity between us. There is perhaps merely a fleeting moment of one person opening to another, nothing more.

My voice is gentle as I speak—not in a seductive way— but in a soothing, earnest tone that my clients uniformly find both comforting and disarming. "How does this feel? Are you ok?"

He nods, and I can feel the tension in his body begin to ease. "Do you wanna tell me why you're here?"

You'd be surprised just how many people come here for something other than sexual gratification. I study his gaze patiently, waiting for the honesty of confession to bubble out of him. "It's been a long time since I've... been intimate with anyone. As you're probably aware, orcs go through mating cycles. And mine is approaching."

Good, but not enough.

"You're a very handsome male, Tharion. You could have gone to any bar or pub and found yourself a mate. Even if only for the night."

His throat works, swallowing back the truth I can sense he needs to purge.

"I don't like one-night stands…"

My hands shift from stroking his jaw to threading my fingers through his long, black hair and grazing his scalp.

"Understandable… Anything else?"

"I guess I'm lonely… Sometimes."

"Well, that's natural… I think most of us feel that way."

His brows pinch. "Even you?"

I nod, answering honestly. "Especially me."

He gives a thoughtful hum. "So how does this work? My friend gave me the list, and I know it was mentioned on Spyder's Web, but it also said that things can vary from Mistress to Mistress…"

"In a nutshell, I will give you pleasure."

His eyes search mine, and I can practically feel his naturally dominant energy pouring out of him. "What if I get the most pleasure from pleasing you?"

My lips tip up in an empathetic smile. "I know the feeling."

Truly. It's what I love most about being a Dominatrix. And I have never met anyone I'm willing to be submissive for because that takes a whole other level of strength that I don't have.

"Unfortunately, that isn't a rule I'm willing to break. There might be other Mistresses here who are willing to reverse roles, but it won't be me, my darling."

Tharion continues to study me silently as I leisurely graze my nails across the back of his neck before he grunts in ascent.

I give a soft tug on a tendril of his hair. "I need your words, little lamb."

A corner of his lips tip up in a grin, mirth sparkling in his eyes, and I meet him with one of my own. This male is anything but a *little lamb.*

"Understood, Mistress Wolf."

I've always rebelled against my given name. I've no idea why my parents would burden me with a soft name in such a cruel world, so I was more than happy to follow suit alongside the Masters and Mistresses, wisely using pseudonyms here at Moth & Flame when I was hired a few months ago. I chose a name for myself that embodied everything I've always wanted to be. So, at least for my appointment hours, I get to be exactly who I want to be.

In a world where I have always felt powerless, I get to be powerful.

LAZARUS

*L*oneliness. It is a disease of the mind. No matter how isolated we may think we are, we are never truly alone. I can feel it in the subtle energies that surround us, whether they be lingering spirits or the lovingly woven threads within this absolutely fucking bizarre tapestry that bind our consciousness within this dimension.

Intellectually knowing this, however, does little to ease the symptoms of loneliness. A disease that plagues us all at some point or another. I am, inarguably, one of the most powerful beings in all of Gothika, and it is all thanks to my so-called gift. A gift that I have spent my entire life trying to get rid of. To stifle, quell, purge, kill.

I cannot touch or be touched without absorbing the other person's magic—their power and life force energy. I am nearly as old as the dirt beneath my feet, and I have travelled to every realm I could find, all to find a power great enough to suppress or eliminate my power, all to no avail. The only people I have ever touched with my own flesh are those I wished dead.

The closest thing I've ever come to a solution was to sever my own arm and replace it with a synthetic one that, thanks to magical and technological advancements, connects to my nervous system and allows me to at least shake someone's hand and *feel* them.

My toes curl into the cool grass beneath me as I stare out into the horizon, where the sun paints its dusky lament as night claims its victory in the sky. Plants and animals are the only living entities whose touch I've ever been able to experience, and it is something I am immensely grateful for, even if I don't understand it. But then again, I don't know much about my magic, where or *who* I came from, only that I am.

"Boss."

The voice of my eldest gollum, Oleander, a creation of my own making, appears at my side. "Mr. Morainu has arrived. Shall I prepare the hydro-carriage?"

* * *

DRAVEN, my oldest friend—my only friend—sits in the plush velvet seat across the carriage from me, studying me with an intensity that only he has the privilege of doing. "Thank you for arranging this…"

I can *feel* he has more to say, but perhaps senses my dour mood and hesitates. Staring out at the towering evergreen trees lining the road, my eyes gradually slide to his as a nostalgic grin curls a corner of my mouth. Many years ago, I'd served as a Reaper beside him for the Blackspire Empire's elite military. Back when I'd been a little more volatile and unrestrained.

"How could I say no to my only friend and confidant when bloodying my hands with you is one of my favorite pastimes?"

Draven's gaze lingers as a frown tugs at his usually stoic

features, telling me that he sees through my mask of nonchalance.

It drags a sigh from my chest. "If you would be so kind as to hasten spitting out whatever it is you're been gnawing on, I'd be immensely grateful. It's turned your aura an unsightly shit-brown."

Draven chuckles. "I just... I want you to know that I'm sorry it took me so long to visit. I was in a dark place for a while and..."

My eyebrow archs, as my eyes drift over the golden energy caused by his laughter to seep into the dark queasy energy pouring further into the space surrounding him.

Not that I need to see his aura to recognize guilt when I can see it carving each line of his features. "... And you were afraid I'd enflame matters?"

"Something like that."

I shrug. "Well, for what it's worth, I'm sorry too. I know it's a two-way street. I'm in a better place now. More at peace."

Resigned.

His features tighten like he can intuit everything I'm not saying.

"I was also thinking that it might be good for you to come visit Moth & Flame."

"I thought business was booming? Or is there someone you need me to dispose of?"

"I think you should come meet my new hire."

My jaw clenches as my annoyance flares. I learned millennia ago not to get my hopes up about *anything* when it comes to romance. I've had exceedingly few relationships, and as soon as they discover why I won't touch them, they run for the hills. And no matter how deranged Draven's latest hire is, they'll be no different.

"I think you should take employee safety a little more seriously."

"In case you've forgotten, she can still touch you if she wears gloves, right?"

I have a long-suffering sigh as he continues, rubbing at my temples with thumb and foregfinger as he continues.

"And not all of it is about sexual pleasure. It's about *connection.* You're depressed because you isolate yourself. When was the last time you spent time with someone whose company you actually enjoy? Hm?"

In initially, my expression is utterly apathetic but soon grows into something heated.

"I don't like people. Why would I not isolate myself from them? As I recall, *you* don't like cantaloupe. Does that mean I should be nagging you to eat more cantaloupe?"

I *will* a cantaloupe into my hands from gods know where or whom I just stole it from, but it's freshly cut and leaking juice over my gold synth hand as I thrust it towards him despite already regretting having *willed* it here in the first place.

"Here, Draven. Have some fucking cantaloupe. I know you hate it, but surely that can be remedied if I just jam it down your fucking throat."

Draven's lip curls at the sight of offensive peachy-orange flesh and stringy seeds that do, I now realize, look rather unsettling. His voice is deathly calm.

"Get that fucking thing away from me."

I roll my eyes and take a large, juicy bite before *willing* it back to wherever it came from and regret it instantly. Cracking open the window to my carriage, I lob the thing out of my mouth.

Draven looks bored. "Happy now?"

Taking a deep breath, my gaze drifts out the window as

my thoughts vier towards the imminent future. The imminent *bloody* future.

"Not even remotely, but in about ten minutes, when Lord Allister *Fuckhole* is relieved of his head, I might find some momentary joy in that. And I have you to thank for it."

CAN'T WAIT FOR BOOK TWO TO ARRIVE?

Gilded Fangs & Mortal Flesh
Coming March/April of 2025
(yes, it will be longer—150-200 pages appx.)

In the meantime, I'd love for you to check out my other
works:

My Blood is Yours
The Summoning Series, Book One
(stand-alone)
A Sweet, Cozy, Highly Explicit/Spicy, Gothic, Fantasy
Romance
Now Available on Kindle Unlimited, Amazon, &
ChiaraForestieri.com
(w/ loads of spicy art!)

A Kingdom of Blood & Magic
Hallowed Fates Series, Book One
Dark Fantasy Romance
(riddled w/ TWs, tread carefully)

Available on Kindle Unlimited, Amazon, &
ChiaraForestieri.com

Blood of Two Crowns
Hallowed Fates Series, Book Two
Dark Fantasy Romance
(slightly fewer TWs)
Available on Kindle Unlimited, Amazon, &
ChiaraForestieri.com

TITLE TBD
The Summoning Series, Book Two
(stand-alone)
April/May
Exact Release Date TBD

Hell Hath No Fury
A Prequel to Hallowed Fates Series
Dark Fantasy Romance
(moderate TWs)
June/July 2025
Exact Release Date TBD

In This Life & The Next
Hallowed Fates Series, Book Three
Dark Fantasy Romance
(moderate TWs)
August/September 2025
Exact Release Date TBD

Wanna see some spicy artwork?
Stay up-to-date with all my upcoming works?
Join my spicy book lovers FB Group,
Courtiers of Carnal Curiosities?

Collab?
DM me?
(I absolutely love to hear from y'all)

Find me on instagram: @authorchiaraforestieri

or

TikTok: @authorchiaraforestieri
(need to invest more time here!)

or
(sorry, last one)

Sign-up for my Newsletter:
https://www.chiaraforestieri.com/epistle-sign-up
*(**BEWARE: NSFW** (explicit) **art included**)*

WANNA SEE SOME *SUPER* SPICY ARTWORK?

Burn thy britches and sign up for my newsletter!

It's hosted by the MMC of whatever book I'm currently working on/promoting so you'll get to have a nice lil one-on-one sesh with them, PLUS XXL peen (among other things) is guaranteed—illustrated by some of the most magically inclined artists in all the realms!

for real, their work is breathtaking, so prepare for your jaw to hit the mothereffing floor

https://www.chiaraforestieri.com/epistle-sign-up

ABOUT THE AUTHOR

@AUTHORCHIARAFORESTIERI

Originally from the US, Chiara Forestieri is a single mother of two [not-so] tiny little love muffins (an 19-year-old and a five-year-old, as of 2025) that spends her days taking care of her small family, practicing Brazilian Jiu-Jitsu and Muay Thai [with the grace of a failing inflatable tube man], pouring her heart and soul into creative and entrepreneurial endeavors, such as this book. All with varying degrees of success, of course. Ranging from 'well, at least no one died' to 'have you lost your mind?'

Currently, she lives in wonderful London, praying desperately for sunshine and warm weather. While many of her prayers have been answered, this one is most often not.

Some of her favourite things (outside of family and friends) include:
- Her Kindle
- Brazilian Jiu-jitsu
- Muay Thai
- All things nature and wilderness
- Animals
- Clean sheets (*drool*)
- Dirty humor
- The sea (her home)
- Hot-warm-and-squishy freshly baked cookies
- Sun
- Kindness

- Cuddles
- A fiery hearth
- Pyjamas
- Oh, and love. Love, love, love. :)

Wanna see more of your favorite characters? See excerpts from upcoming books? Or just general juicy, steamy, roman-tasy content?